John-Paris Kent lives in
three children. He hasn't k   ʋɪ
ages but in 2011 his story *Fi*   ᴄommended
by A.L. Kennedy at the Bric   .ɪᴢe. In 2013 his poem
Ex-Girlfriends was also shortlisted by Roger McGough.

Where I End

John-Paris Kent

PRINTED BY SARSEN PRESS

A catalogue record for this book is available from the British Library.

© John-Paris Kent
First published Spring 2023

ISBN 978-1-7398332-7-5

Designed by Tim Underwood   timund@hotmail.com
Cover artwork by Chloe Kent
Printed by Sarsen Press   22 Hyde Street, Winchester, SO23 7DR

Contents

WHERE I END

On Holiday

How do you look into
someone else's eyes
and let yourself be tender

       without losing everything?

How do you talk about sunsets
which people forget
are the movement of the fucking earth

       without breaking down?

How do you even get out of your chair?
Saying "I love you" is easy.
Showing the fear of an ordinary heart

       is death itself.

Ex-girlfriends

My ex-girlfriends
are all thinking about me
right now.

I know it.
I can feel it.

Wherever they are
whatever they're doing
they're thinking about me.

They all met me
they all know how fantastic I am –

that's why I still pop up in their thoughts

although,
to be honest
I'm pretty tired

so I think I'll just go to bed early tonight.

Driving Home

It is me: not a
forty-five year old
listening to Hank Williams
and Bach, driving home.

But I am forty-five:
and I am listening
to Hank Williams
and Bach, driving home.

The Past

Driving past the pub
                        where I met my first girlfriend

I feel suddenly breathless

the simple fact of my own past
pinning me back
with its hand on my throat

a shape, with sides –

a physical thing
wedged between me in my car
and the pavement where
we first spoke.

I am still alive
she is still alive
I am married
with three children
she is married
with three children

but the centrifugal force of now
is refusing to let me take off my seatbelt.

The past is flat-pack –

assembled from screws
and washers
in sealed bags

and it is always laid out
    before us –

demanding to be put together.

Honey

"It's OK, honey. I'll just pause it. Take as long as you like…"

"Ah. OK. Cool. Thanks. How do you have it again?"

"White. No sugar. Thanks, honey."

Twice. Fuck. That's way too much. And I'm not her fucking honey. Jesus. We sound like Terry and June. But we're not even funny.

His legs were a bit stiff from sitting on the sofa and he shook each one separately, as if getting rid of crumbs, before going over to the counter. He breathed in deeply. It wasn't quite a sigh; but he needed it. She'd come over to watch a film. It was Sunday night. Perhaps the second or third they'd spent together. But it was the first time they'd consciously decided to just 'stay in'.

Although he'd come through to make tea he didn't put the kettle on immediately. Instead he just stood there, staring, but the shiny metallic surface prevented any other thoughts from forming.

Honey. Oh God. Why does she have to call me honey? It's so naff.

An image of Terry's big face came into his mind. Grinning that dirty, sitcom grin.

Or was it a grimace? Although, actually, June was alright really. Quite trim. Quite smart. What the fuck are you thinking? June Whitfield was alright. What the fuck is that?

He remembered the Christmas special he'd watched last year. He'd watched it by himself, on TV Gold or something, and enjoyed it. Up to a point. Terry's boss had come round. And made an embarrassing speech at the dinner table while they were all wearing silly paper hats.

Shit. What if we end up married? Right. You'd better start.

Just put the kettle on. That'll give you a few more minutes. You can't do this. You really can't.

He flicked the switch and stepped back. Then he opened the cupboard door right in front of his head and took out two cups.

Matching cups? You can't use matching cups. But it's even worse to take out two different ones on purpose. Please. This is ridiculous.

Terry's big face appeared again. Then someone from a Carry On film. Both were middle-aged. Both were obsessed with sex. Both should never have got married.

He took out two tea bags and put them in the matching white cups and then started biting his nails. Lightly at first. Then more intensely.

Think of all the girls that have been on that sofa. And there she is now. Just through there. Right now. The latest. I wonder what she's thinking? I wonder what she'd say if she knew?

Steam was just starting to come out of the spout.

Dump her. You have to dump her. You don't even want to have sex. Surely you should at least want to have sex with her? If this is it. If this is really it.

He rubbed his face in the palm of his hands.

"Do you want a hand, honey?"

OK. That's it. Even her bloody voice is suburban.

"No, thanks. It's OK. Nearly done."

So how are you going to say it? I guess you'll just have to go in there and spit it out.

Terry's gormless face appeared again. This time it was huge. And that laugh he had. That laugh that knew the whole world was against him.

Is that what happens? It will be unless you do it. Now. Today. She's lying on the same sofa you had Emma. And Martha.

Emma and her pink knickers. Remember how she whispered it that first time? And Martha. Fuck she was hot. Turning up drunk and getting you to talk to the cab driver. In a short skirt. They must've loved her at that work thing.

OK.

His hand hovered over the handle as the kettle came to the boil.

OK. Just say it. Just say it.

A bit too much water came out into the first cup so he had to pour a bit into the sink after dabbing the tea bags. He then went over to the fridge and got out the milk.

OK. This won't be nice. She really likes you and, yes, you will be lonely. And you'll be on your own. For a while. But you can't lie. You really can't. This is much, much worse.

He opened one of the tins on the counter and put a spoonful of sugar into one of the cups and stirred it slowly. He then shut his eyes and took another deep breath.

Each cup in each hand felt heavier than he'd expected. And the living room door had closed behind him so he had to push it open again with his foot.

She was still on the sofa. But she was sitting at the far end like a child waiting for her piano teacher to come in and take her through for a lesson.

He also noticed that she'd moved her bag, which she'd dumped on the floor just inside the door when she came in, just as she always did.

"Listen, honey…" she said.

The Troll

The first door I tried didn't open. We were standing on the decking outside but it was probably too early in the season, and too wet. "This place really does look shit."

"Well, you booked it!"

"How was I meant to know? Anyway, the other one was full."

Looking inside my heart sank. The tables were all set – each knife and fork wrapped in a yellowy-orange napkin – but it already seemed inevitable that no one would come. The stone floor had also been mopped but nothing else looked as if it had been moved or touched for years. The display of old books on the shelf probably had a layer of grease and dirt on it that would wipe off on your finger. And the small selection of magazines looked so random they almost made me want to gag.

Peering in through the glass panes in the door I had the same feeling I get in all guesthouses in British seaside towns: a bottomless sadness that can only be cured by leaving.

The decking was wet, which darkened the colour, and there were at least six or seven of those standard pub tables with bench seats along the sides. They all still had their parasols up, although some were tilting quite badly, and the ashtrays were all half-filled with rain water.

We walked round to the front, which was on the road. There was a proper hanging pub sign and one of the double-sided billboards on the ground advertising 'Home Cooked Food' but the moment we went in the sinking feeling came back: only doubled.

There was one person with his back to us sitting at the bar and generic pop music was playing in the background,

I presumed from the jukebox in the corner. There was also a faint smell of disinfectant in the air and at the far end of the bar, just inside the hinged bit you raise to get in and out, an unhealthy-looking man in his fifties was reading a book in the mid-afternoon light. "Hello. How can I help you?"

He took off his half-moon reading glasses – that really didn't suit him – and put down his book, splaying the pages out on the bar. From the cover it looked like a thriller but even though the author's name was written in large thriller-type font I could only read half of it – 'Angela' something. I wondered how long he'd been reading before we came in. "Hi, yes. I think we've booked room for the night?"

I'm not sure why I said 'think'. I was pretty sure; and I'd written it down on our itinerary. Maybe I was hoping they'd been a mistake.

"OK. What's the name please?"

"Kent. Mr Kent…" Somehow the 'Mr' also seemed to be way of maintaining our distance.

"Let me just have a look here. Yes, here it is. Mr Kent. One night."

"Yes, great."

"OK. Hang on a sec and I'll show you to your room."

It was later that night that Simon first called him 'The Troll' and it stuck: he had a lumbering, breathless walk that meant I had to keep slowing down behind him; not quite a limp but an uneven, heavy tread that made me think he had a bad knee or something. He was wearing a red polo shirt with some sort of logo on the front, possibly something he'd had made up as a kind of uniform – the type that has a really high polyester count – and he was overweight and almost bald.

As we walked back across the patio he took some keys out of a loose pocket in his trousers. "I'm afraid I've had to put you in Room 1. It's still a family room but with a bunk-bed rather than two doubles."

I was level with him now and he looked up at me briefly as he spoke. We didn't really make eye contact but I remember feeling disgusted, not just by his proximity – by the implied intimacy of walking side by side – but also by the defiant edge in his voice. He knew he was shafting us – he knew the room wasn't as nice – and he knew it was his fault.

"Oh what. Really? Bunk-beds? That's really not good."

"Sorry, but I'm afraid there's been a cancellation. Sometimes it just happens like that."

"But that's really not what we've paid for..."

It was the first time we really looked at each other: the anger in his face had made it swell with patches of ruddy white, like when you press your finger hard against your own skin, and when he spoke again his whole head seemed to shake. "As I said it's still a family room. There's a double and a bunk bed."

"But – "

"It's OK. Honestly. A bunk bed is fine. I don't mind. I'll sleep in it. It's fine. Really."

As The Troll unlocked the ugly brown door which obviously led up to the second floor Simon gave me a look behind his back, as if to say 'What's wrong with you?'

It opened onto some carpeted stairs and as we followed him up a smell that I couldn't quite place got stronger and stronger until it was almost overpowering. At the top I realised what it was: aftershave; strong, male and cheap.

This time the door was open. It was just after eight in the morning, a bit earlier than we'd said, but he was there again as we went in. The lights weren't on yet and it looked like he was still wearing the same red polyester polo shirt as the day before. "Morning. Help yourself to cereal. Full English?"

The question was almost too much for him to carry so early in the day. And as he said the last two words his eyes betrayed an achingly fragile hope that they at least might allow us all some mutual certainty.

We took the table right in front of the bay window which looked out onto the road. There was a painted concrete block directly opposite, with a little metal plaque saying 'Public Conveniences', but it wasn't an unpleasant view: there was also some nice planting in the flowerbeds and some cute cottages further up the hill which, nearer the top, was thick with pines and some other trees I couldn't identify.

Inside, on the wall nearest us, there was a framed but badly faded poster of an old stone balcony. The writing underneath said: 'Juliet's Balcony, The Basilica, Italy'. I looked round the rest of the room. The tables were all still set in exactly the same way except I noticed there were also single, but quite large, dried flowers in small vases on each one (how much easier, I thought, to use dried flowers than real ones.)

A sinewy, small-headed man that we hadn't seen before came up to the table. "Morning. Sleep OK?"

It felt weird being asked how I'd slept, and I felt embarrassed on his behalf.

"Would you like some toast?"

"Please."

The sound of frying had already started in a kitchen that was somewhere out of sight and the small-headed man came back out very quickly with a little basket of brown toast.

And it was him again that bought out the breakfasts.

"Enjoy."

It started almost immediately after he must've finished cooking. And it made us both stop eating. Each one was a deep raking tear – the sound of the same phlegm being dragged up again and again and again – and it was coming from outside, just to the left of the window.

"Jesus. The Troll really isn't well."

"No. That's not good. And it's really putting me off this sausage."

"Shut up! Don't say anymore…" and Simon shuddered as if to underline his repulsion.

We'd decided to pack before breakfast so when he emerged again I told him we were ready to pay. Simon said he'd go and get the bags so I followed The Troll back through to the bar. As I walked behind I noticed he also had a slightly deformed elbow: the skin was a bit darker and the bone itself stuck out at a funny angle.

He opened up the hinged part of the bar and reached up for a hard-backed black and red book on the shelf while I stood in front, feeling faintly silly about resuming my position as a customer so formally.

He put on his glasses and opened the book. There were fine light blue and red lines dividing the page into rows and columns. He scanned down with his finger. "Mr Kent. There it is. That'll be sixty pounds please."

Once the payment had gone through I went back out onto the patio – all ready to go – but Simon still wasn't down. The thing is The Troll came out too – as if carrying out some sort of proprietorial duty to 'see us off' – and so, for a brief moment, in Simon's absence, we were both forced to stand there on the patio alone.

"Well, I hope you get better weather today."

"I'm not holding out much hope…"

"Oh, I don't know you might be lucky. If you look over there there's a few patches of blue sky coming…" He pointed up with his Troll-like hand at the end of his Troll-like arm and together we looked at the sky just above the hill. He was right: light patches of blue were indeed just beginning to break through. "It might not be sunny but it's certainly muggy. I'm sweating like buggery."

Suddenly I felt so glib. And so cruel. I have absolutely no idea what has happened to him in his life. And, to be honest, I have no idea what's going to happen in mine either.

And in that moment I hated myself.

Just like he did.

Humans

Who are we, us humans?

Why aren't we sniffing
each other's arses?

And humping in the street like cattle?

We dress in front of mirrors
and talk on the phone

but through shoe
through sock
and through pavement

we, too

walk on a planet
that spins.

Love

I saw a middle-aged
couple kiss, once, towards
the end of an evening

in a pub. And pressing
his lips on hers
the weight of both their experience

was beautiful in its need
and in the practicality
they were willing to share.

Filament

I don't know why I decided to clean the kettle. It wasn't even dirty, apart from a few water stains. At first I just used a sponge. But that made it worse. So I picked it up.

It felt jaunty and light but as I took it over to the sink I remembered I'd recently bought some of those sachets you can get that remove limescale.

I checked. There was indeed an unopened box under the sink.

I took one out and chopped off the corner. I then pushed across the tap and started filling the kettle with cold water. When it was virtually full I turned it off.

The kettle was heavy now and I had to stiffen my wrist to stop it spilling. I put it down and, pressing lightly on the sides, poured in the contents of a sachet.

The water frothed and spat furiously, like the finale of a fireworks show.

I put my face right up close.

All around the filament millions of frenzied little bubbles were dissolving a crust of calcium that had built up over God knows how long. It was beautiful: they were ravaging it; stripping it down without thought or conscience.

I watched for a least a minute. Maybe three or four.

After a while, though, it started to die down and as I stood, listening to a stupid echo inside my kettle, I suddenly understood exactly what she'd said.

And I closed my eyes. Like they do after you're dead.

The Washing

I love the fact that you can
hang clothes out to dry.

Imagine if you couldn't?

Humanity would be smothered under a pile
of its own wet washing.

At the Urinal

Trigonometry with the floor
and work shoes

colleagues; people who work
in the same building

men: with wives, children, partners
perhaps even a moped

lined up to face the firing squad.

Silence. Then brazen puffing

absorb; de-clench; let go

Red Arrows soaring with self-consciousness
with wing mirrors of anxiety

but with love, too.

Three wrinkled appendages
stuck in a rut together.

Homeless

I saw a homeless man asleep on the street yesterday
                              as I walked home from work

he had his right hand stretched out on the pavement
                    as if he was doing front crawl

and his left hand tucked between his legs.

I do that, too.

Plant

They got out of the
Vauxhall together,
one on each side –

then crammed into
my hallway as I
closed my flat door.

It was just after Christmas,
and mum held forward
a plate that I recognised
covered tightly in film.

I made a fire, and showed
them round, but my dad
is old now, and it was
raining, so we looked at
my garden from inside.

He clutched the sill
next to me and his noisy
green coat was quiet.

"I like that plant," he said.
"I like the way it catches
the drops in its leaves."

Pruned

I would love to be pruned

hard

my straggly-leaders
cut right back to the base
on an afternoon in January
and left to wait for the cold.

Handfuls of sappy growth
executed by secateurs.

Clip.

Right there!

At last,
at last.

Memory

We were sleeping on the top floor
while work was being done on the house.

The dust settled on everything.
The sheets were sticky to touch.

And I listened to Aretha Franklin
(you were in New York)
an album all the way through.

You at the backdoor in a headscarf,
and new lipstick

this season's colour.

A kiss on the lips

me,
in the garden
playing a role.

A generational change.

I said that to mum,
on Wednesday.

She will be gone one day, and so will dad –

but I am a cuckoo
        and you're in my blood.

Blazer

Putting on a blazer
hauls me up
from the silt of the morning –

a fast-dripping wreck
suspended by crane

ready to be swung round
and brought ashore
with mechanical certainty.

Commute

My commute begins

with a trolley
of anxiety –

beers, wines and crisps

dragged
backwards

by a low-paid employee

down
the
aisle
of
my
sleep.

The smell of my work shirt
a shaved face –

black shoes

that
only
I
know
are
uncomfortable.

A ticket from
A to B.

The tracks of our minds are private
but we are cargo –

I
screw
up
my
ticket
and
put
it
in
the
same
clear
plastic
bin
24-hours
later.

The annulment
of time

in my loose trouser pocket.

Rainbow

I went out like a snail
with doubt on my doorstep
getting looks, imagined or not

but the green was so green
the wet was so wet
the rain uneven and brash

a perfect half-circle
unnatural and dead
as a crow shook the rain

off its back.

Negative Voice

It takes anything –

a
sorting
office
for
the
slightest
of
doubt.

Why didn't you think of *The Gruffalo*?

A
letter
from
my
nearest
and
dearest

sucked
into
a
chute

and
then

thump

on
the
welcome
mat

that I always leave out.

Thanks for that.

Yes,
thanks.

Maybe
I
am
deluded?

Maybe
I
am
starting
to
make
a
bit
of
a
fool
out
of
myself?

Maybe I should just shut up?

Give up

you
say?

Even better.

A
pat
on
the
back.

Thanks.

Thanks
so
much
for
looking
out
for
me.

Witness for the Prosecution

She called me. Twice. First while my phone was off. Then again as we were walking back from the restaurant. OK. I didn't answer. But you have to admit that's not bad. In fact, I'd say it's pretty fucking conclusive.

That's easy. You texted her earlier that same evening, didn't you? So it's no surprise she called you back. She was just being polite...

But twice? That's more than just being polite. And she was never going to call first anyway. Especially after what I said last time. The ball was in my court. That's why it had to be me that texted her. And that's why-

Your Honour. I think the witness is deviating from the point. I'm really not sure what this has to do with the case...

Upheld. The witness must answer questions directly. You are being cross-examined about your claim that Gemma has changed her mind. This is not about how you feel. We know that already. So please, continue, bearing in mind what I've just said...

Sorry, Your Honour. Where was I? Ah, yes. She called me. Twice. Well, three times if you include Saturday. Now would she have done that if she wasn't interested? I think not. And to call me at ten-thirty, Your Honour. Quite late, you have to admit. That must mean something. She was almost certainly getting ready for bed...

OK. It's Friday night and there you are, walking back from the restaurant with Rhiannon. It's ten thirty. Your phone rings. It's Gemma – and yet you don't answer. May I just ask why?

Why? That's obvious. Because Rhiannon was right next to me.

And why was that a problem?

Well, you know, it would've been awkward. Difficult. You know.

So. You'd rather have spoken to Gemma without Rhiannon being there? Perhaps at another time?

Yes, exactly. What's wrong with that?

Nothing. Nothing's wrong with that. That makes perfect sense. And do you know what Gemma was doing earlier that Friday night? Before ten-thirty? Before she called you? Have you considered the possibility that she may also have been 'busy'? After all she's a very good-looking girl. And it wasn't just Friday night, was it? It happened again on Saturday, didn't it? Except on Saturday her mobile was actually switched off. And don't forget there's absolutely no point lying because –

It was switched off because she's depressed. That's why. She's depressed because she hasn't seen me for nearly two months and she's finding it hard to cope. And that's why she called me so late on Friday, too. She's unstable. She's suffering. She just wants to tell me everything – to let go – but she's too scared. I know it. I just know it.

Have you not considered the possibility that her phone was switched off because she didn't want to speak to you? Just like you didn't want to speak to her on Friday night. I mean you've feared all along, haven't you, that she would meet someone at that wedding. She would've been looking very sexy in that 'orange dress' she told you she'd be wearing. And you know what weddings are like. You've done it yourself. Especially Santorini in the sun. Do you really think she was thinking about you all the time?

I object, Your Honour. The prosecution's tone is aggressive and unjustified and whether or not she was looking sexy in an orange dress at a wedding I didn't even go to in Santorini with people I don't even like is pure conjecture anyway.

32

Upheld. May I ask the prosecution where you're going with this line of questioning?

I'm simply making the rather obvious point that if Gemma was looking sexy at the wedding then surely it follows that she was more likely to 'pull' – to use the modern vernacular – or more likely to have 'been pulled', which would completely rubbish the defendants claim that she actually loves him.

OK. I will allow you to continue but please refrain from this aggressive tone. The defendant is defending himself – and indeed prosecuting himself – without having had any formal training. It's your job to disprove the case being made; not to question his wider character.

I understand, Your Honour. So. Getting back to Saturday afternoon – the afternoon of the conversation – do you now accept that if Gemma was spending the day with someone else – perhaps someone she may have met at the wedding – she may also have turned her phone off to avoid having to speak to you?

No. She turned her phone of because she's depressed. She can't face it. I told you that already.

But you have no proof for that, do you? No proof whatsoever. And, in fact, on Saturday, when you did speak to her, she sounded fine, didn't she? Dare I say, even happy?

But she's never done that before. She's never turned her phone off. That must mean something. This is a completely new situation. For both of us.

Of course, this is a new situation but that's exactly –

Did you hear that? He just admitted it! He just admitted it! This is something new! And he just admitted it!

Please. All parties must refrain from shouting in court. This is no way to conduct yourself. Calm down immediately or I'll be forced to have you removed.

I'm sorry, Your Honour. I just got a bit carried away. Please.

Sorry. Can I just mention something else – something very specific – from the actual conversation. What about that joke she made about my sexuality? You know when she said "…and you're straight!" after that silly little anecdote I told her. I mean what's that if not her recognising my sexuality? And don't forget this is all now after she – how shall I put this – after she saw my penis. What am I saying? I fucked her for God's sake. She grabbed my hand and put it right inside her pyjama bottoms – right on it – saying "Why did you stop?" What more do you want for fuck sake? What more do you want?

I'll allow this to stand because I can clearly see how much this means to the defendant but no one is questioning the fact that you had sex with her…

Twice!

Yes, twice, in France, two months ago, but again I repeat: you are being cross-examined about your belief that she loves you and, indeed, not only wants to be your girlfriend but also to marry you and have a family with you.

OK, yes, I do understand that, but… yes, OK. But when I spoke to her yesterday I got the feeling… oh fuck. Fuck. Why did she do it? Why? OK. She loves me. She doesn't love me. OK. That's not the point. The point is that she might. Yes. She might. Hang onto that. She might. In fact I'm sure. And it's OK. It's been worse. It's been worse. But… what if she really doesn't like you? Again.

It hurts in your tummy doesn't it? Deep inside. You know, really, don't you? Why don't you just let it all out…

But my hand was right on it. Her pussy was all mine. It was right there in my hand. Right here. All the little bits. Forever. So easy. So easy. And what about when I kissed her tits? All of sudden there they were. Fifteen years. Fifteen years. Then once. Twice. And gone. Just gone. A top, just a top – some material –

that's all there was between me and her tits. A top. £19.99. And I took it off. Then her bra. I saw her bra. I saw it. I saw it.

You won't see it again though. Will you?

But I touched them. And kissed them. I kissed her tits. I heard her make that noise – slowly, deeply, beautifully – breathing in my ear – a real sex noise: me; me and her; us; we; together; having sex; making love; in France; on the floor; her breathing; my breathing; so close; so real. And wasn't there a third point? Something else? There was. I know there was. Something so sure. Undeniable. Please. Please. What was it? What was it? Come on. That's it – wait – deep breath – slowly, think back… she called you, orange dress, no, not that, she called you, yesterday, in the garden, her voice, something new, there was something new… yes! "We'll hook up soon." Yes! We'll hook up! You will see her again. Just wait. That's it. Trust. Trust. That's it. My closing argument. What will happen will happen. No – it's not quite that – you will see her – you'll want her – of course you will – and she might – that's it – she might – if you let her – if you leave it – she might. She did before. Her tits. You saw them. And it might happen again. It might.

Beyond reasonable doubt?

Right. That's it. I'm getting up. No more of this shit. I'm getting up. The alarm's about to go off anyway…

Is it? Well why don't you have a look? Why don't you just open your eyes and have a quick look? It's right there. And that way you'll know. Won't you?

Four Kings

"I think you should apologise."

"What?"

"I think you should apologise."

"What for?"

"For the fact that hundreds of thousands of people have been killed." Simon was calm and deliberate, in that way of his.

"Don't be stupid."

"In fact – we all think you should apologise."

"Look. We've been over this before. I'm not going to apologize. I've got nothing to apologize for."

"What about the fact that millions of people are now dead despite the fact that there weren't any WMDs. And the fact that the Middle East is now more fucked up than ever before. And the fact that you're a cunt."

"Whether I'm a cunt or not is beside the point. Look, I really don't want to get into this again. Let's just play. Who hasn't called yet?"

I badly wanted to say something. Just a "come on" or something to shut Simon up but I couldn't because then they'd all know.

"I think Simon's right, Ben…" Ralph's voice was gentle and contained but – as always – his sensitivity was obvious all over his face. "I think you should apologise. To all of us. Right now."

My stomach tightened. Ralph was sitting next to Ben but he'd now turned his shoulders so he was facing him directly.

"Yeah, Ben. Be a man." Ant chipped in too and then reached across and grabbed the packet of rolling tobacco from the middle of the table and started making a cigarette.

"Look. We've been over this hundreds of times and it's really starting to get boring. We're here to play poker. So let's just play. J.P.? Who's go is it?"

The two kings facing me looked like credit cards in someone else's wallet. And the two on the table looked almost embarrassed. "Not mine…"

"Ben. The reason I want you to apologise is simple: you got it wrong. Badly wrong. And the reason we keep going over it is because you never do. Just like Tony Blair you refuse to accept any responsibility for the fact – and it is a fact – that you supported, listen – supported – an invasion based solely on the assumption that Saddam was a threat. And I don't care what you say now. That's how Blair justified it and that's how you justified it Ben. And you know it."

"Look. I've told you before I supported the decision because I thought it was right. And – yes – of course I accept now, with hindsight, that there aren't any WMDs. Of course I accept that. But – as I've also said before – it wasn't just about WMDs. But I really don't want to get into that now. Right. Someone – Ant – let's have the turn. Come on baby. Let's see it!"

"What do you mean it wasn't just about WMDs? I haven't heard you say that before…" Ralph's tone was reasonable; but his intensity wasn't disguised.

Ant lit his cigarette. The straggly bits sticking out of the end flared up almost comically in the flame.

"Let's have the tobacco, Ant…"

"No. Don't give it to him until he answers." Simon put his arm out just as Ant was about to slide it over. He was wearing a green-tinted plastic visor – as a joke – and a jumper which made him look like his dad.

"For God's sake, Simon. Don't be a cock."

"No really, Ben. I haven't heard you say that before. What do you mean it wasn't just about WMDs? What else was it about then? I'm interested to hear…"

Ralph now had his elbow on the table. And he'd put down his cards.

"What is this? What are you trying to prove, Simon?"

"I'm not trying to prove anything, Ben. I'm just asking you to do what most people do when they're wrong. Accept responsibility. And apologise."

"Ant. Give me the tobacco."

"No, Ant. Don't."

"What's the other reason, Ben? What's the other reason you supported the invasion?"

He didn't answer again: we were in his house; in his front room; at his table; Marilyn was away, and we were meant to be playing poker.

"Ant. Please pass me the tobacco."

"No, Ben. Not until you either explain or apologise." Ant's face was resolute, but he seemed to think this was just the usual banter.

"Ant. This is my house. Give me the fucking tobacco. "

Simon raised his arm again like a level-crossing.

"Are you fucking mad? What are you doing? What the fuck are you doing?"

Everything was happening too fast. I couldn't catch-up. And the secret of my cards suddenly felt unbearable.

"Move your arm, Simon…"

He didn't. And the look on his face was disgusting. One I've never seen before. Smug. Arrogant. Scared. Nasty.

"Simon. Move your arm…"

Simon's face didn't move. Neither did his arm.

"I swear Simon, if you…"

"Ca…

"JUST FUCK OFF!"

I'll never forget the tears in Ralph's voice as he looked up. "Why don't you ever say something JP? Why don't you ever say something?"

Birdsong

In my middle years
I've started to take more
of an interest in birds,
and birdsong –

I noticed it suddenly
waiting for the train one day

when I saw him, or her

standing on the branch
laden with blossom

and thought

What on earth you are saying?

The Willow by the Pond

It was twilight at the pond and he felt all eras were in him
in his presence.

The ducks were all going in the same direction across the
reddening pink sky.

There was movement on the surface: paddling feet, feathers
all getting ready for bed.

It is just before dark but the willow hadn't moved for hours,
days, years

the not quite yet black silhouette of the trees and the black
of the water.

He felt the cold air as he took off his scarf and on his head
without a hat.

He could hardly see but he wasn't scared.
It was thrilling

the reflection of willow branches in the water, gentle ripples
so still

and the way the branches never quite touch the surface. He stood
listening to the ducks.

Their silly noises. Playground quacking. What is so profound
about the willow?

Why is it so mournful? It looks at its reflection like a
dying elephant

watching us as we come and go. Mention the way its leaves
hang down, he thought

like weaving. And as the wind blew up and he heard
the other trees

he suddenly knew what it was: the willow never gets to rustle
its own leaves.

Judgement Day

To the counter, a lifetime
offered in exchange –

a list of addresses,
a date of birth,

the whole of my life
for a nod, for a word

pull the quilt round your ears
but don't give it a name –

your empire of self,
and a lifetime of pain.

Mountain

You win,
brutal thumb of rock.

I can feel my teeth
loose

in their sockets –

peaked serviettes of hard
but not as hard as human hate.

I could scratch your eyes out
with a turned face.

Shadows can't slam doors

and your boulders are just
Lego bricks that I tread on –

looking for something else.

Ice on the Lake

I can't stop thinking about
the ice on the lake,
over my shoulder
still there when I close my eyes –

by evening it was all
smudged by fun
but the snowballs still have
no weight

and the flatness is
still spreading

like blood

on a kitchen floor.

ing

The things I experience –

a warm evening
the smell of cooking
voices, light, warmth

the coolness of the fountain
I breathe emotion into me

the sound of heels
car tyres, a bird
two people talking
traffic lights changing
the silhouette of a tree

the taste of coolness
the taste of surprise

of ripeness, of rotting
the taste of my future
of lust, churns my soul

the memory of every moment
fills me with love and pain

constant movement
the noise of the city

engines, horns, intentions
histories, living forwards
going home, going out

going, looking, feeling

but a gentle breeze brings
tears to my eyes and I stop:

a girl on a bike rubs her eyes
a waiter is taking a tray back in
the old man by the railings doesn't move
boys laugh on the zebra crossing

a man waiting at the lights
changes the angle of his head
and moves his hands on the steering wheel
as a woman walks past with a file
and a seductive walk

the metal shutters outside
the pharmacy are closing

she is seconds late
the church bell chimes

carrying, walking, talking

no one is a stranger anymore.

A Glass of Water

He went back into the kitchen to fill his glass with water because she was now in the bathroom. And as he passed the closed door he could hear she had the taps on, quite full.

There were two small steps in his corridor and he walked up them deliberately because he hadn't turned the lights on. After a few more steps he reached round the open door of the kitchen and switched on the light without needing to look.

He was naked and there was a slight chill in the air. They'd had a fire in his living room but he hadn't put the heating on so the rest of his flat was still quite cold. He could feel the floorboards under his bare feet and seeing his own body beneath him in the bright kitchen light made him shiver.

This is me, he thought. My body. He didn't dislike it – and in fact it felt complete and balanced because he'd played football earlier. His muscles felt used. And he could feel the strength he still had. His penis hung down below his pubic hair and the hair that was getting more and more bushy on his stomach around his belly button. He noticed that vein along the side and the way his penis just dangled, limp and lifeless. We're all just animals really, he thought. But rather than feeling any disgust, he actually found the idea quite comforting.

He had the glass in his hand and he moved carefully forwards towards the sink. He never lowered the blind on the back door and, although all the lights in the houses on the other side of his garden were off, he still didn't want to be too blatant.

It had been raining and he could smell the damp outside. He turned the tap and held the glass until it was full, keeping his legs bent, again, just to make himself feel he wasn't being too cavalier.

There was a bit of a draft coming up through the gaps in some of the floorboards and, as he turned away from the sink, he noticed their diner plates exactly where they'd both left them on the table. His knife and fork looked extremely graceful, just overlapping slightly, almost like a young girl's curtsy; on her plate the fork was strewn at an angle on the plate and the knife was on the table. The bowl of pasta was still where he'd put it down to serve and the metal serving spoon, crusted now with hard bits, was sticking out to the side. There were two empty wine glasses. And the bottle of wine, which he wasn't quite sure whether they'd finished. Behind that the apples and lemons in his fruit bowl looked abundant in the way they tumbled over each other. There was also a basil plant he'd bought from the supermarket and some Italian cabbage from the organic shop down the road. And in the bottom of the salad bowl two pieces of lettuce were just beginning to wilt and darken in colour.

He heard the toilet flush in the bathroom. And in the glass in the backdoor he saw the reflection of the bathroom light go out. He then heard her open the door and imagined her getting back into bed and pulling the quilt up round her ears.

He stood there a moment longer. He could feel the wood under the soles of his feet. The water in the glass was transparent and clear. And it wobbled slightly on the surface.

This is enough, he thought. You are happy.

And suddenly he realised that he felt like crying.

Citrus

You bear your soul
with the patience
of a Christmas bauble

but you are more
than a fruit –

you are a coagulation of leftover colour

an old man's elbow
showing us the way

and if we only knew better
we would just

wink at you,

and smile.

Paradise

Russell looked over at his girlfriend. She squeezed his hand in hers and smiled with her mouth closed, understanding. She knew exactly what he was going through.

'This is it,' he thought. 'When we land everything changes. *Everything*.' But he didn't say anything either. He just kept starring forwards at the synthetic material on the back of the head rest in front of him.

The plane lurched sideways again. He could tell the palms of his hands were really sweaty now but he still didn't move. Then a bump. Up and down. Then another. Each jolt thinning the air but thickening his determination; which was now almost a solid object.

They were making the final descent. And what must've been *at least* five minutes ago the pilot had reassured everyone that despite the "bumps on the way down" they would be landing in ten minutes time.

He tried to feel the life they had. To feel the everydayness of it all. Up there, at however many thousand feet. The certainty of getting up and of going to bed. Of going to work. Of the pub opposite. Of Jack. Of Tom. Of Sally. Of putting his own shoes on. Never again would he be so flippant about life. About the simple fact of it. Never again would he waste so much time. From the moment the plane landed he would live every moment. Every dull, grey moment like it was a step on the ascent to heaven.

Another drop. His stomach was left behind. Then the whole plane shock; the big plastic monster he was now strapped into just because they'd bought tickets on a website a few months ago.

He thought of the bolt he'd studied earlier through the

window when they were cruising above the clouds. The little cross-head one on the wing. This shouldn't be flying. I shouldn't be flying. Why? Why do we have to explore? The human race should stay on the ground. We are *not* birds. Why can't we just accept what we are? Why can't we be happy with what we've got?

Somewhere on the plane a lever or a flap moved that made a noise. A mechanical noise. An engineered noise. An unnatural noise. His reflex took over and he looked round at the window as if to get his bearings, to check everything was still OK, that they weren't plunging, but all he could see was thick billows of cloud being thrown past the window as if they were on some sort of cheap film set.

And he could tell by the tight silence that everyone was now in this together. OK. Just count. One. Two. Three. So different. I will be so different. So utterly different.

Maybe you could even get rid of your phone too? Imagine that. No more messages. No more texts. No more doing things just because of everyone else. He would live how he wanted to live. How we should live. And a shimmer of cold excitement flowed through him at the mere thought of such a bold decision. And what people would say.

Another bump. A shallow one this time. But rattling. The one that might finally work something loose.

Chloe had her eyes closed. She looked serene, and beautiful. And no more moods. No more introspection. Awkwardness. Or comparing.

He glanced out of the window again and for the first time saw a quick patch of ground. Ruddy and wet and profoundly disappointing; but paradise. Utter paradise. He craned over and Chloe opened her eyes. She didn't say anything but gave him a gentle kiss on the arm. "I love you."

"I love you too, baby."

It's that simple. It really is that simple. Come on. Nearly there. Nearly there.

He could see the tops of houses now in lines and patterns unappreciated from below. The plane was still being buffeted from side to side but it seemed to know where it was going now and his blood was rising. Individual cars. And trees. Just seconds. Just seconds. But it would still be bad. Fire. And… Stop. Deep breath. One… Two… Three… Four…

The plane banked downwards again and he pictured the pilot with a big gear stick; pulling it backwards.

Then suddenly, sooner than expected, that jolt.

That's it. Wait. No. Yes. That's it. Wait. Wait. The flaps on the wings went up on each side and as the rushing noise took over elation spilled over inside him. Hope and love for everything and everyone almost blinded him. He was down again. On the ground. Through his leg, the plane, the wheels, the rubber – the earth.

Thank you, God. Thank you. I won't forget this. This is it now. This is it.

"Well," Chloe said, taking his hand and squeezing it hard. "We made it."

The plane was now taxying along the runway and as it turned left a member of the cabin crew made the standard announcement asking people to remain seated until it came to a complete stop.

Russell was delighted to obey out of sheer gratitude but as the plane straightened and then taxied alongside the terminal, he noticed that quite a few people in the seats around them were now turning on their phones. And as he stood up a few minutes later and reached up into the overhead locker he wondered whether he, too, might have any new messages.

Halfway

She still jiggled her legs. Not in a nervous way but playfully, like an excited child, as if she was playing peekaboo or something under the table – open, shut, open, shut, open, shut – right from the ball of her hips. And they still looked great in jeans. What's that word they used in the Fifties? Pins. Two long, sexy pins.

It was Anna's birthday the first time I met Maxyne. And it was Anna's birthday again. She'd sent the email out ages ago – 'A lazy Sunday in the pub? (oh yeah, and it's my birthday!)' – but the moment I saw her name in my inbox I thought of Maxyne. My first reaction was guilt (is this really my first reaction to an email from an old friend?) but it soon lifted and whenever I was on my own over the following few weeks – perhaps walking from A to B, or waiting in a queue – I found myself flirting with the mathematical probability of whether or not Maxyne would actually be there; considering all the factors I could think of in detail, both known and unknown.

The day itself was a bit of a rush, even though it was a Sunday. I was staying with dad while mum was away for a few days playing her violin in Italy with a new group. I was being 'a good son' but I didn't mind. In fact, I was enjoying it. I like spending time with my dad. More than just like. Quite frankly there's nothing more important in my life and I know he feels the same. Dad is old now (I actually just wrote 'quite old' but took it out). Dad is old. Old. Old like an old person. My five-year-old niece calls him Pa, as in Grandpa. And I guess she's the only one in the family who really sees that. To me he's always dad. Like the other day in the hospital. He was in for two days because he'd had breathing problems again in the night and when me and mum arrived to visit he was asleep on the hospital bed, on his side, wearing one of those spearmint-coloured smocks they give you. And as he turned to push himself up it all gathered up around him and his white belly fell out a bit and I could see his shiny white shins. People think intimacy is about sex. It's not. It's seeing someone asleep and I'd never seen my dad asleep before – apart from when he was just a terrible snoring mass under the covers in their dark bedroom when I used to go in after a bad dream.

Even though mum was away he was perfectly happy for me to leave him that night – "You don't want to be stuck in here with me all night" – and, in the end, I think I left about six. I wanted to start thinking about Maxyne the moment I closed the front door but it felt a bit childish and rude knowing dad was still just metres away through the wall behind me so, as a compromise, as I walked down the steps and onto the street I decided to try and work out exactly how many years it was now since that nine months we spent as 'boyfriend' and 'girlfriend' without either of us actually using the words. It must've been the second year after university; that period when everything we all talked about was new. Anna was playing some of her records at a grungy pub in Old Street the night we first met, and I'd gone along with David. I remember feeling good that night. Physically. Like all my energy was contained within me. I even remember the shirt I was wearing – that faded green denim one with poppers at the front that always felt a bit clunky and stiff – but I was feeling so good I could even override that. I can also remember exactly – like I can still actually feel it in my hand – what it felt like to put my arm round her waist for the first time. The beautiful curve of her middle through her top. And I remember lying awake later that night in David's angular spare room just looking at her name and number in my phone.

There was only one free chair when I arrived, which was at Anna's table, so I went straight to the bar without looking back. Maxyne was there but I had no idea whether she'd seen me or not because she was on a different table and she was looking the other way. After buying myself a drink I took the free seat and tried to care about Anna and her presents. I even ended up talking to some trendy-looking guy with heavy black-rimmed glasses that Anna apparently used to work with. He was really nice – genuine and smart – and he even asked for my email address – but every word I said had to be forced out. All I could think of was the fact that I couldn't turn round without being rude and so when I felt a tap on my shoulder it really made me jump.

"Hello, stranger. Do you still smoke?"

"Hi!" I said. "No. But I'll happily come for a fag…"

"Typical!"

The day outside was the same day it had been: light clouds moving quickly across the sky as if they were being wound on invisible wires. And we stood in the doorway just off the pavement so it was sheltered; but it was still quite cold.

She offered me a Malboro Red. And lit mine before even taking one out of the packet for herself.

"So, how've you been?" I asked.

"Oh, you know. Same old, same old. I've got a new dog, though, and he's amazing. He can jump over two times his own height! Like a flea!"

We both smoked two in a row and I asked just as we were about to go back in.

"That'd be nice," she said. And she smiled in a way she'd never done before.

In the end, by email, we decided on a 'posh burger' after work rather than lunch; and she picked the place. It was called Byron and it was near her new flat in Islington (the one she bought after we spilt up). It was Thursday night, a week and a half later, and we agreed to meet at eight. I was early, as usual, but I didn't mind. It gave me a bit of time to settle in and look at the menu and when a Converse-wearing waiter eventually came over it felt nice to be able to say I was "just waiting for someone."

I even got up and walked over to a table near the back, looking for a paper to read. There wasn't one so I picked up one of the little pamphlet things that were on display. 'That's just about the best burger I've ever had. Giles Coren.' Normally that 'just about' would've really annoyed me – why couldn't he just say the best burger? – but this time it didn't. The pamphlet was full of great reviews and there was even an email address for people who might want to 'join the team'. I might tell Maxyne I was considering a career change, I thought. It might be quite funny. And suddenly just the chance, or even just the thought of the chance of what might happen – seventy per cent? Eighty per cent? – was so over-whelming I had to close my eyes.

It was definitely her kind of place and as I sat down again I realised that, if I was honest with myself, I also liked, and even respected, the way they were trying to get an authen-tic American diner feeling going. I liked the squeezy plastic mustard bottles and the laminated menu. 'Proper Burgers' they promised. It was a good choice.

At five past eight she texted saying she was going to be

a bit late, blaming the tube and the fact she had to take her dog home first. But I still didn't mind. In fact I liked her even more. Before, she would've just showed up at half past. At least now she was letting me know.

"I don't love you." That's how she said it. Not even "I don't think..." or "I'm not sure..." We'd just been shopping on a Saturday morning. Somewhere I'd never been before. I'm not sure why. Or for what. Maybe we've both grown up a bit, I thought. Maybe, I thought. Just maybe.

I looked out of the window on my left. It was a narrow cobbled street. The kind it costs millions to live on. God, I was so upset that day. That Saturday when I couldn't think of anything else. And for weeks after. If only I'd known. I could've just done anything I wanted. Been instantly 'over it'. Imagine that. But so much has happened since then, I thought. Three hundred and sixty five days times nine (or was it ten?) has happened. Hundreds, thousands of days all filled with my life: that thing I'm always so concerned about.

I have to say it was a really nice evening. Nicer than I'd even hoped. She was wearing a fantastic stripy top, with colours like a crayon set, and tight black leggings. Her freckles were out (she said she'd just been on holiday, quickly adding "with Ingrid") and her work seemed to be going well. After a while we got into a debate about why I don't like the Guardian and that was cool too; not mean, but kind of flirty and informed at the same time. She still drank a bit more than me – and I wasn't too sure about her bloody dog – but it felt good. Not weird. Or sad.

A bit later she started talking about using her Wii to get fit and I made a joke about wearing a green leotard like the Green Goodness. She said she'd probably just wear "my knickers" and I felt so horny I almost felt dizzy: but

I'd already decided I wouldn't even try and kiss her that night. Whatever happened. This time I would wait. You've changed, I kept thinking.

After dessert (I had a Knickerbocker Glory) we went outside for the first fag of the evening. There were two chairs and a small table right on the pavement, like it was Greece or something, and we had to wait as two groups of people both tried to pass in opposite directions at the same time. It was cold, though, and we both needed our coats.

First we talked about how many of our mutual friends were now married with kids, running through a list and verbally ticking them off like a school register. Feeling strong still, and in control, I then decided to ask – outright – about the long-term boyfriend I knew she had after me. After she'd told me about it, and why they'd split up, she then asked me about Erin.

There was a pause after I finished speaking and as we both pulled our coats tight around ourselves I suddenly felt like we were two very separate people. Part of me wanted to stand up and give her a hug; but I didn't. And as the moment passed she spoke again. "I'm desperate to get married," she said. "And have kids, if someone will have me…"

As we hugged to say goodbye, squeezing each other really hard at least three times, I told her how much I'd enjoyed it and said we should "definitely" meet up again soon. But as I walked away, and back down the High Street, I realised that if I didn't call or email her I might never see her again. Ever. And as I waited for the lights to change, so I could cross the road and turn left towards the tube, I had the unnerving feeling that I'd just reached the exact halfway point of my life.